# Enid Blyton

# Christmas in the Toyshop

For further information about Enid Blyton please visit *www.blyton.com*

ISBN 978-1-84135-596-2

First published as *Oh! What a Lovely Time* by The Brockhampton Press Ltd 1949

This edition entitled *Christmas in the Toyshop* published by permission of
Chorion Rights Limited

First published by Award Publications Limited 2002
This edition first published 2009

Published by Award Publications Limited,
The Old Riding School, The Welbeck Estate,
Worksop, Nottinghamshire, S80 3LR

www.awardpublications.co.uk

09 1

Printed in China

# Enid Blyton
# Christmas in the Toyshop

*Illustrated by Sue Pearson*

AWARD PUBLICATIONS LIMITED

Once upon a time there was a toyshop. It sold sweets as well as toys, so it was a very nice shop indeed.

All the children loved it. They used to come each day and press their noses against the window, and look in to see what toys there were.

"Oh look at that beautiful doll!" they would say. "Oh, do you see that train with its three carriages – and it's got lines to run on too."

"Look at the rocking-horse. I do love his friendly face!"

"Oh, what a lovely shop this is! When we grow up let's keep a shop *just* like this one!"

Miss Roundy, the shopkeeper, liked having a toy-shop. She liked seeing the children and showing them all her toys, and she nearly always gave them an extra sweet or two in their bags when they came to spend their pocket money. So, of course, the children all loved her.

The toys loved her, too.

"Look – she found me a new key when mine dropped behind the shelf and couldn't be found," said the clockwork train.

"And she put a spot of red paint on my coat where some got rubbed off," said one of the toy soldiers. "She's very, very kind."

The toys liked living in Miss Roundy's shop till they were bought by the children. It was fun to sit on the shelves and the counter, and watch the boys and girls come in and hear them talk. And it was very exciting when one of them was bought, and taken proudly away by a child.

The toys didn't like Sundays as much as weekdays, because then the shop was shut, and nobody came to see them at all. They couldn't bear it when Miss Roundy took her summer holiday and shut the shop for a whole fortnight! That was dreadful.

"It's so *dull*," complained the biggest teddy bear, and he pressed his middle to make himself growl mournfully. "There's no one to see and nothing to do. Miss Roundy even pulls down the window-blind so that we can't see the children looking in at us."

And then Christmas time came, and the toys had a shock. Miss Roundy was going to close the shop for four whole days and go away to stay with her aunt. Oh dear!

"Four days of dullness and quietness and darkness," said the rocking-horse, gloomily. "Nothing to do. No one to come and buy us, or see how nice we are. Four whole days!"

A black monkey with a red ribbon around his neck

spoke in a high, chattering voice.

"Can't we have a Christmas party for ourselves?"

"It's an idea," said the rocking horse, smiling. "Let's all think about it until Christmas comes – then we'll have a GRAND time in here by ourselves!"

The day came when Miss Roundy was going to close the shop. She pulled down the big window shade. Then she turned to the watching toys.

"I'm going now, toys," she said. "I won't see you again for four whole days. Be good. Merry Christmas to you – and try and have a good time yourselves. Do what you like – *I* won't mind! Merry Christmas!"

She went out of the shop and locked the door. The toys heard her footsteps going down the street.

"Merry Christmas, Miss Roundy!" said everyone, softly. "You're nice!"

And now they were all alone for four days. *What* were they going to do?

The toys did what they always did as soon as the shop was shut for the night. They got up and stretched themselves, because they got stiff with sitting so long on the shelves and counter.

"That's better," said the rag doll, shaking out her legs one after another to loosen them.

The pink cat rolled over and over. "Ah – that was good," she said, standing up again. "I do love a roll."

The little clockwork train whistled loudly and the toy soldiers climbed out of their boxes and began marching to and fro.

"Nice to stretch our legs a bit," they said, and then they scattered because the roly-poly man came rolling along, not looking where he was going, as usual.

"Look out," cried the captain of the soldiers, "you'll bump into the dolls' house! There he goes, rolling to and fro – what a way to get about!"

"Listen, everyone!" called the rocking-horse. "Let's talk about Christmas."

"When is it?" asked the big teddy bear.

"The day after tomorrow," said the rocking-horse. "I think if we're going to have a good Christmas ourselves we ought to make our plans now, and get everything going, so that we're ready by Christmas Day."

"Oh yes!" cried everyone, and they all came round the rocking-horse. What a crowd there was. All the little dolls' house dolls, and the other bigger dolls, the skittles, the railway train with its carriages, and another wooden train, and the roly-poly man, and … well, I couldn't possibly tell you them all, but you know what toys there are in a toyshop, don't you?

"Sit down," said the rocking-horse. And everyone sat, except, of course, the things that could only stand, like the trains and the motor cars and the balls.

"We shall want a party," said the rocking-horse. "That means we must have things to eat. We can take any of the sweets and chocolates we like, to make into cakes and things – Miss Roundy said we were to help ourselves."

"We can make the food," said the dolls' house dolls.

"We'll help," said the skittles, excitedly.

"We can cook on that nice toy stove over there," said the twin dolls. One of the twins was a boy doll and the other was a girl doll, and they were exactly alike.

"The pink cat and the black monkey can arrange a circus," said the rocking-horse. "They'll have great fun working together on that."

"I'll do the Christmas tree," said the clockwork sailor. "We'll have presents for everyone under it! We'll play games afterwards, too."

"What a pity Father Christmas doesn't know about us!" said the roly-poly man. "It would be so nice if he came to the party."

"I don't suppose he'll be able to come," said the black monkey. "He's much too busy at Christmas time. Don't roll against me like that, roly-poly man. You'll knock me over."

The roly-poly man rolled away and bumped into a row of soldiers. They went down on the floor at once. As they got up and brushed themselves down, they shouted angrily at the roly-poly man.

"Don't let's quarrel," said the rocking-horse. "People should never quarrel at Christmas-time. It's a time to make one another happy and glad. Now – to your work, everyone – and we'll see what a wonderful Christmas Day we will have!"

The dolls and the skittles set to work at once. The doll with golden hair and the twin dolls took charge of the cooking. They got the little toy cooker going, and there was soon a *most* delicious smell in the toyshop – the cakes were baking!

There were chocolate cakes and fudge cakes and peppermint buns. There were little jellies made of the jelly sweets Miss Roundy sold. There was a very big iced cake with tiny candles on it that the rag doll had found in a box.

The baking and cooking went on all day long. The twin dolls had to scold the roly-poly man ever so many times because he would keep rolling against the golden-haired doll just as she was taking cakes out of the oven.

Still, as you can see, there was plenty of everything.

"What a feast we are going to have!" said the rag doll, greedily. "Ooooh – fudge cakes – I'll have six of those, please, on Christmas Day!"

The clockwork sailor did the Christmas tree. He was very, very clever. He climbed right up to the topmost shelf, which Miss Roundy had decorated with evergreens, and he chose a very nice bit of fir.

"Look out!" he called. "I'm going to push it off the shelf." So everyone looked out, and down came the little branch of fir tree, flopping on to the floor.

The clockwork sailor climbed down. He did a little dance of joy when he saw what a wonderful tree the bit of fir would make. He wondered what to put it in.

"If you'll get me out of my box, so that I can join in the fun for once, you can use my box," said the gruff voice of Jack-in-the-Box.

The toys didn't really like Jack-in-the-Box very much. He lived inside a square box, and when the box was opened he suddenly leapt out on a long spring, and frightened them very much. The clockwork sailor didn't really know if he wanted to get Jack out of his box.

"Go on – just this once,"
said Jack-in-the-Box.
"I promise to be good.
I'll perform in the circus,
and be funny if you like."
   So Jack-in-the-Box
was taken out of his box
and he wobbled everywhere
on his long spring, enjoying
his freedom very much.

The box was just right for the Christmas tree. The clockwork sailor filled it with earth that he took from the pot that held a big plant belonging to Miss Roundy. Then he planted the bit of fir tree in it.

"Now to decorate it!" he said. So he got some tiny coloured candles and some bright beads out of the bead box, and some tinsel from the counter, and anything else he could think of – and dear me, the tree really began to look very beautiful!

"I can make a star to go on the top of the tree," said the teddy bear, and he ran off to find some silver paper.

"And now you're none of you to look," said the sailor, "because I'm going to pack up presents for you – yes, a present for every single one of you!"

The circus was practising hard. There were two clockwork clowns in the toyshop, so they were exactly right for the circus. They could go head-over-heels as fast as could be.

"We want some horses," said the black monkey, who was very busy. "Pink cat, stop prowling round the cakes, and see how many horses you can find."

The roly-poly man said he wanted to be a clown, so the teddy bear made him a clown's hat, and let him roll about the ring, knocking people over. Jack-out-of-his-Box jumped about and waggled his head on his long neck. He was really very funny.

The pink cat borrowed some horses from the soldiers and the farm. She led them down to the circus ring.

Noah arrived with his animals from the ark. There were elephants, lions, tigers and even kangaroos!

"It's going to be a GRAND circus!" said the pink cat. "Oh, hurry up and come, Christmas Day!"

Well, Christmas Day did come at last! The toys rushed to one another, shouting "Happy Christmas! Happy Christmas!" at the tops of their voices.

The railway train whistled its loudest. The big bear and the little bears pressed themselves in the middle and growled. The musical box began to play, and the rag doll sat down at the toy piano and played a rollicking tune.

Nobody knew she could play and they were all very surprised. So was the rag doll. She hadn't known either, and once she had begun to play she couldn't stop! So what with the engine's whistle, the bears' growling, the musical box's tunes and the piano there was a very fine noise.

The roly-poly man got so excited that he knocked over two of the horses, rolled on the monkey's tail and upset a jug of lemonade.

"Can't you stop rolling about and be still for a moment?" said the pink cat, keeping her tail well out of the way.

"I can't stand still," said the roly-poly man, "because I've got something very heavy at the bottom of me. It makes me wobble, but not fall over. I really will try to be good – but if you were as wobbly as I am you'd find it difficult, too."

The black monkey suddenly appeared dressed up in white trousers and a top hat! He carried a whip in his hand. He cracked it and made everyone jump.

Then the pink cat appeared, carrying a drum. She beat it – boom-diddy-boom-diddy-boom-boom-boom. "The circus is about to begin!" shouted the black monkey and he cracked his whip again. "Walk up, everyone! The circus is about to begin!"

"Boom-diddy-boom-diddy-boom!" went the drum.

All the toys rushed for seats. The black monkey had arranged bricks of all sizes and shapes out of the brick-boxes for seats and there was room for everyone. The dolls' house dolls were allowed to be at the front because they were so small.

The skittles were so excited that they kept giggling and falling over.

"Quiet there! Settle down please!" shouted the monkey. "Pink cat, sound the drum again – the performers are about to march in."

The circus began. You really should have seen it. The horses were splendid. They ran round the ring one way, and then turned and went the other way.

Then the clowns came on, with Jack and the roly-poly man. The roly-poly man rolled all over the place and knocked all the clowns over. Then the clowns tried to catch Jack, but they couldn't, of course, because Jack sprang about all over the place, on his long spring. The toys almost cried with laughter.

The elephants were cheered when they came in. They waved their trunks in the air and trumpeted as loudly as they could. The lions and tigers came in and roared fiercely. The kangaroos jumped all round the ring and the bears walked in standing up on their hind legs.

All the toys clapped and cheered and stamped at the end, and said it was the very best circus in the world. The pink cat and the black monkey felt very proud and they stood in the middle of the ring and bowed to everyone so many times that they really made their backs ache.

"Now for the tea party!" called the doll with golden hair. "Come along! You must be very hungry, toys – hurry up and come to the party!"

What a wonderful tea party it was! There were little tables everywhere. In the middle of them were vases of flowers that the dolls had picked out of the dolls' hats that Miss Roundy kept in a box on a special shelf.

The tables were set with the cups and saucers and plates out of the boxes of toy tea sets. There was a tea-pot on each, full of lemonade to pour into the cups.

The cakes were lovely. There were fudge cakes, peppermint buns, chocolate cakes, all kinds of biscuits, toffee sandwiches, jellies that wobbled like the roly-poly man and, of course, the Christmas cake was the best thing of all.

"We've put it on a table by itself, because it's so big," said the golden-haired doll. "I hope there'll be a slice for everybody."

It looked lovely. The golden-haired doll had decorated it with icing. Everyone thought that was very clever indeed.

The pink cat ate so much that she got fatter than ever. The captain of the soldiers lent the twin dolls his sharp sword to cut the cake. The roly-poly man rolled up to see them cutting it, and nearly got his head cut off!

When nobody could eat any more, and all the lemonade was drunk, the skittles cleared away. "We'll wash up and put all the tea sets back in their boxes," they said. "The rest of you can play games."

So, whilst the skittles were busy, the toys played party games. They played blind man's buff, and the blindfolded pink cat caught the elephant out of the Noah's Ark.

"Who can it be?" wondered the pink cat, feeling the elephant carefully. All the toys laughed, because of course, they knew who it was.

They played hunt the thimble, and nobody could see for a long time where the thimble was hidden. Then the clockwork sailor gave a scream.

"The captain of the soldiers is wearing it for a helmet – he is, he is!"

And so he was. He was sorry to give it up because he thought it was a very nice helmet indeed.

The trains gave everyone rides, and so did the toy motor cars. Even the aeroplane said it would fly round the nursery once with everybody. The musical box played hard for anyone who wanted to dance.

The roly-poly man made everyone laugh when he tried to dance with the rag doll. He rolled about so much that he knocked everyone off the floor.

They were all having such a good time. Then suddenly they noticed that all the candles on the Christmas tree were alight!

"Oh, oh! It's time for the Christmas tree!" cried the toys, and they rushed over to it. "Isn't it pretty? Look at the star at the top!"

"Where's the clockwork sailor?" said the roly-poly man.

"Gone to fetch Father Christmas, he told me," said the rocking-horse. "Do you suppose he meant it?"

And then, will you believe it, there came the noise of bells!

"Sleigh bells! It really is Father Christmas coming!" cried all the toys, and they rushed to the chimney. "He's coming! He's coming!"

Down the chimney came
a pair of legs – then a pair
of red trousers – and then
with a jump, down on the
rug came a merry,
white-whiskered fellow,
whose red hood framed
his jolly red face.

"Father Christmas! You've come, you've come!" shouted the toys, and they dragged him to the tree.

"Wait a bit – I want my sack. It's just a little way up the chimney," said Father Christmas. So the big teddy bear fetched it. It was a nice big bumpy-looking sack.

"Happy Christmas, toys," said Father Christmas. He was a very nice *little* Father Christmas, not much bigger than the dolls. The toys were glad. They would have been rather afraid of a great big one.

"Happy Christmas!" sang out everyone. Then Father Christmas undid his bag. Oh, what a lot of things he had! There were ribbons and brooches for the dolls, sweets for the soldiers, chocolates for the Noah's Ark animals, and balls, made of red holly berries, for the toy animals. Nobody had been forgotten. It was wonderful.

Father Christmas handed out all the presents, beaming happily. Then he took a few presents from under the tree.

"These are special presents for the people who tried to make your Christmas so nice," he said. "Presents for the golden-haired doll and the twin dolls – and for the black monkey and the pink cat – here you are, special little presents for being kind and good."

"But what about the clockwork sailor?" said the rocking-horse, at once. "He did the tree, you know. Have you forgotten him?"

"Where is he?" said Father Christmas.

Well, dear me, he wasn't there! Would you believe it?

"I saw him last," said the rocking-horse. "He said he was going to fetch you, Father Christmas. *Didn't* he fetch you?"

"Well, I'm here, aren't I?" said Father Christmas, and he laughed. "Dear me – it's sad there's no present for the clockwork sailor, but I don't expect he'll mind at all."

The toys had opened all their presents. Somewhere a clock struck twelve. Midnight! Dear dear, how dreadfully late!

The twin dolls yawned loudly, and that made everyone yawn, too.

"We'd better clear up and go to bed," said the golden-haired doll. "Or we shall fall asleep on our feet, and that would never do."

So they cleared up, and in the middle of it all Father Christmas disappeared. Nobody saw him go. The pink cat said she saw him go into the dolls' house, but he wasn't there when she looked.

Somebody else was, though – the clockwork sailor! The pink cat dragged him out.

"Here's the sailor!" she cried. "Here he is! Sailor, you missed Father Christmas – oh what a terrible pity!"

But, you know, he didn't! He was there all the time. Have you guessed? He was Father Christmas, of course, all dressed up. He had climbed up the chimney when nobody was looking. Wasn't he clever?

"You were Father Christmas!" cried the golden-haired doll, and she hugged him hard. "You're a dear!"

"Yes, you are," shouted the rocking-horse. "That was the best part of all, when Father Christmas came. We were so sad there was no present for you. But you shall have one – you shall, you shall!"

And he did. The toys threaded a whole lot of red holly berries together, and made him the finest necklace he had ever had. Look at him wearing it. Doesn't he look pleased?

Miss Roundy will never guess all that the toys did in her toyshop that Christmas Day, will she? If you ever meet her, you can tell her. I do wish I'd been there to see it all, don't you?